Ladybird books are widely available, but in case of difficulty may be ordered by post or telephone from:
Ladybird Books – Cash Sales Department Littlegate Road Paignton Devon TQ3 3BE Telephone 0803 554761

A catalogue record for this book is available from the British Library

Published by Ladybird Books Ltd Loughborough Leicestershire UK
LADYBIRD and the device of a Ladybird are trademarks of Ladybird Books Ltd

DISNEY

Pinocchio

Name: Sally bunton
Age: 32

Ladybird

Hello there! My name is Jiminy Cricket.

Do you believe that if you wish upon a star your dreams come true? I bet some of you don't. Well, neither did I until something quite extraordinary happened. Let me tell you about it.

Once, in a small Italian village, there lived a man called Geppetto. He was a very good woodcarver.

Geppetto made all sorts of toys. Each one was beautifully carved out of wood. Cuckoo clocks, musical boxes, clowns, animals and puppets filled the shelves of his tiny shop.

One cold wintry night, I took
shelter in Geppetto's workshop.
As I headed towards the warm fire,
something caught my eye. There
on the workbench sat a wooden
puppet. He was Geppetto's latest
toy and he was nearly finished.

7

I watched Geppetto take up his paintbrush and carefully paint in some eyebrows and a mouth.

"See! That makes a big difference," said Geppetto to Figaro, his little cat. "Don't you think so, Cleo?" he asked his goldfish.

Then, turning to the puppet again, Geppetto cried, "Now, I have just the name for *you* – Pinocchio!"

That night, as Geppetto
settled down to sleep, I watched
him glance out of the window.
"Look, Figaro!" he cried,
pointing to the brightest star.
"It's the Wishing Star…

Star light, star bright,
First star I see tonight,
I wish I may, I wish I might,
Have the wish I make tonight."

Geppetto closed his
eyes and whispered longingly,
"I wish my little Pinocchio was
a *real* boy." Then he sighed and
went straight to sleep.

As the night went on, silence fell over the village. The stars twinkled at one another and shed their soft light over the houses. One ray of light fell into Geppetto's workshop. I woke with a start. The light sparkled and swirled, and out of it stepped a beautiful Blue Fairy. I could hardly believe my eyes.

14

The Blue Fairy glided across the room towards Pinocchio. "Geppetto is a good man and deserves his wish," she said softly.

"Little Puppet made of pine,
Wake! The gift of life is thine!"

And with a wave of her magic wand, the puppet opened his eyes and began to move his arms and legs. "I can talk! I can walk!" he shouted joyfully.

"If one day you prove yourself brave, truthful and unselfish, you will become a real live boy, no longer made of wood," the Blue Fairy explained to him.

"A real live boy!" repeated Pinocchio, in awe.

Then the Fairy turned to *me*,
Jiminy Cricket. Now, I could
hardly believe my ears!

"Will you promise to teach
Pinocchio right from wrong?"
she asked.

I agreed – and was delighted
to find myself suddenly wearing
a brand new set of clothes.

Pinocchio and I soon became
good friends.

With a flutter of her delicate wings, the Blue Fairy disappeared.

The noise had wakened Geppetto, and he got out of bed. He was astonished to find his puppet talking and moving. "Am I dreaming?" he wondered, lifting Pinocchio in his arms. "It's my wish… It's come true!"

Geppetto was so delighted that he began to sing and dance for joy. Even Cleo and Figaro joined in the celebrations.

The next morning, after breakfast, Pinocchio heard voices in the street. He opened the front door and saw the village children hurrying to school.

"They are your schoolmates," explained Geppetto, handing Pinocchio his schoolbooks. "You must hurry now or you will be late."

With an apple in one hand and his schoolbooks in the other, Pinocchio skipped down the street, and I hopped cheerfully behind. Pinocchio turned and waved to Geppetto.

"Goodbye, son," called Geppetto. "Hurry back."

Pinocchio walked happily through the village, quite unaware that he was being watched by two very suspicious-looking characters.

"Hey, look, Gideon!" exclaimed Foulfellow, the fox, to his friend. "A wooden boy! A live puppet without strings! Now, he could be worth a fortune to someone. Let's sell him to Stromboli, the famous puppeteer."

As Pinocchio came close, Foulfellow put out his cane so that the puppet tripped and fell to the ground.

"Oh, I'm terribly sorry!" said Foulfellow, helping Pinocchio to his feet. "I do hope you are not injured."

"I'm all right," said Pinocchio, and picked up his apple and books.

Foulfellow stared at Pinocchio's belongings. "I'm going to school," explained Pinocchio proudly.

"School! That's not the easiest road to success, you know," said Foulfellow. "You should be in the theatre. With your splendid looks and personality, you are a born actor."

"But I'm going…" began Pinocchio.

"…to be a star, with your name in lights," finished Foulfellow. "Come on! Let's go straight to the theatre."

And, with that, the evil pair hurried Pinocchio off down the street.

30

I ran quickly after the three of them.

"Hey, Pinocchio! Where are you going?" I shouted.

"Jiminy, I'm going to be an actor!" cried Pinocchio excitedly.

"No! I'm supposed to tell you what is right and wrong, and this is *wrong*," I cried. But Pinocchio took no notice. So I decided that I had better go to the theatre, too.

Pinocchio was welcomed warmly by Stromboli, and I secretly followed them into the puppeteer's caravan.

I could see Stromboli gleefully rubbing his hands together at the thought of how much money he could make with this puppet without strings.

That evening, Stromboli introduced Pinocchio to his audience. "Ladies and Gentlemen, I now present something you will refuse to believe – the only puppet who can sing and dance without strings. The one and only… Pinocchio!"

The spotlight fell on Pinocchio, and he began to sing and dance. The audience were delighted. They clapped and cheered, and showered him with golden coins.

Meanwhile, Geppetto had prepared supper and was waiting for Pinocchio to return. But as it grew later and later, Geppetto began to worry. "Where can he be at this hour?" he asked himself.

Eventually, Geppetto put on his coat and picked up a lantern. "I'd better go and look for him," he sighed. Then he stepped out into the street, followed by Figaro.

"Pinocchio! Pinocchio!" cried Geppetto, but no one replied.

Back at Stromboli's caravan, Pinocchio was pleased with his night's adventure. But now he wanted to go home and tell his father about it.

Stromboli was furious when Pinocchio told him. "You belong to *me* now," roared the puppeteer, and he locked Pinocchio in a cage.

Later that night, I found Pinocchio crying sorrowfully. "Don't worry," I said gently. "I'll soon get you out of there."

As I struggled with the lock, a dazzling blue light suddenly filled the wagon.

"It's the Blue Fairy," I cried, and I watched her step towards the cage.

"Tell me, Pinocchio," the Blue Fairy asked. "Why didn't you go to school?"

"Go on! Tell her the truth," I whispered. But Pinocchio wouldn't listen.

"I was kidnapped by two monsters with big green eyes," lied Pinocchio.

"And where was Jiminy?" the Blue Fairy asked quietly.

"Oh, he was put in a sack," said Pinocchio.

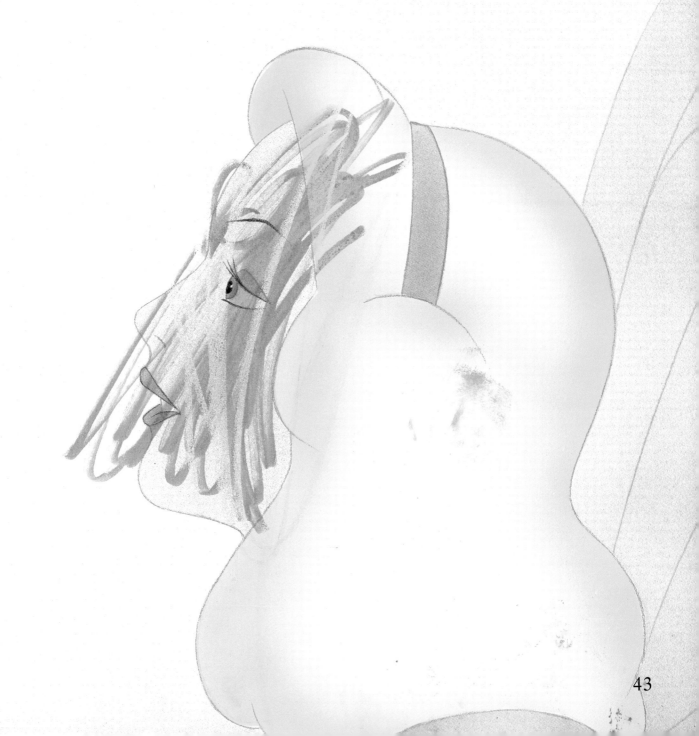

With each lie, Pinocchio's nose grew and grew, until it stuck out through the bars of the cage. Pinocchio cried out in terror.

"You see, Pinocchio, a lie grows and grows until it's as plain as the nose on your face," the Blue Fairy explained.

"Oh, I'll never lie again," pleaded Pinocchio.

The Blue Fairy saw that
Pinocchio was truly sorry.
"I'll forgive you this once. But
remember – if you want to
become a real boy, you must
prove yourself worthy."

She waved her magic wand
and the cage door flew open.
Then the Blue Fairy just
disappeared.

"Come on, we're free!" I cried,
leaping down from the cage.
I hurried Pinocchio away from
the caravan.

Meanwhile, at a nearby inn, Foulfellow and Gideon had found another chance to make some money. They listened eagerly as a wicked coachman explained his plan.

"I collect stupid little boys," said the coachman. "You know, the disobedient ones – and I take them to Pleasure Island. They make silly donkeys of themselves and never return home. Now, here's where you fit in. You bring me some boys and I will pay you with plenty of gold!"

"Yes! Yes!" cried Foulfellow, as he and Gideon chuckled.

Just outside the inn, Pinocchio and I were on our way home.

"I'll race you!" I cried, dashing ahead. Pinocchio began to run, but suddenly a long cane reached out and grabbed him.

"What's the rush, Pinocchio?" asked Foulfellow, tipping his hat in greeting.

51

"I want to get home," explained Pinocchio. "I had a terrible time with Stromboli."

"You did?" said the fox. "You must be a nervous wreck! Here, let me check your pulse." Foulfellow grabbed Pinocchio's wrist. "Oh, my goodness! Just as I thought. You need a holiday. Pleasure Island is just the place for you!"

"But I can't go!" Pinocchio protested.

"Of course you can. Look, here's a ticket," said Foulfellow, handing him a playing card. And, with that, the two rascals led Pinocchio away.

I followed anxiously at a distance, wondering what was going on.

Pinocchio was handed over to the coachman, who was waiting at the edge of the village. Seeing the stagecoach filled with laughing, chattering boys, Pinocchio happily climbed on board.

With a crack of the driver's whip, the stagecoach started on its journey.

That night, they crossed the sea by ferry and landed on Pleasure Island. The boys ran eagerly towards an enormous amusement park.

Once on the island, Pinocchio made friends with a boy named Lampwick, who told him all about the pleasures in store. "No school, no police, plenty to eat and drink. And it's all free! Boy, I can hardly wait!"

All the boys ran riot, and stuffed themselves with food.

"Being bad's a lot of fun, isn't it?" cried Pinocchio, filling his mouth with sweets.

Meanwhile, I, Jiminy Cricket, had been searching desperately for Pinocchio among the crowds. "There's something phoney about all this," I murmured. "I must get him out of here."

Once all the boys were inside the park, the coachman ordered the gates to be closed. Then, looking towards the carnival, he muttered, "Those boys will soon make donkeys of themselves." And he broke into a fiendish laugh.

Eventually I found
Pinocchio playing pool with
Lampwick.

"Pinocchio! You will never
be a real boy if you act like this!"
I cried. "Come on home this
minute!"

Lampwick stared at me,
then laughed. "You don't take
orders from a grasshopper, do
you, Pinoke?"

I was furious, and prepared to fight Lampwick. But Pinocchio protested, "Jiminy, he's my friend!"

"All right. Go ahead and make donkeys of yourselves," I shouted and stormed off.

As I marched out of the room, I could hear the boys still laughing. "Anyone would think something bad was going to happen to us!" sneered Lampwick. But at that very moment, two donkey's ears sprouted from his head!

Pinocchio was horrified. As he stared, he saw a tail grow on his friend. Then Lampwick's feet turned into hooves.

Suddenly Lampwick's laugh turned into a bray. Startled, he glanced into a mirror. There was a donkey staring back at him!

Just then, Pinocchio himself sprouted two long donkey's ears. "Help! Jiminy! Help!" he shrieked in terror.

Hearing Pinocchio's cries, I dashed back inside. "Come on, quick! Let's get out of here!" I yelled, and we raced away.

"Hurry!" I shouted, as we ran across the now-deserted island. "Hurry, before you get any worse!"

Pinocchio ran as fast as his little wooden legs could carry him. He was terrified.

Finally we reached the edge of the island, where steep cliffs overlooked the sea.

"You've got to jump!" I cried, and we both leapt down into the water.

The current took Pinocchio and me to the mainland. We scrambled ashore and rushed back home. But when we got there, Geppetto was nowhere to be seen.

Amazingly, a dove flew overhead and dropped a sheet of paper at my feet. "Look, a message!" I cried. "It says your father has been swallowed by a whale called Monstro."

"I'm going to find him, then," cried Pinocchio, and he headed back to the sea.

Once there, and with a large stone to weigh him down, Pinocchio began to search the ocean. Trying hard to keep up, I raced along behind.

Suddenly a dark shadow loomed across the ocean floor. It was Monstro – and he was looking for some lunch! In a flash, Pinocchio found himself being sucked into the whale's gigantic jaws, along with a whole school of fish. But *I* was left outside in the water, clinging to a bottle.

Pinocchio was swept deeper and deeper inside the whale. At last, in its great cavern-like belly, Pinocchio saw a boat. A sad, forlorn figure sat fishing over its side. It was Geppetto!

"Father!" shouted Pinocchio, grabbing hold of the end of Geppetto's fishing line. "Here I am!"

"What? Pinocchio! My son!" cried Geppetto, taking him in his arms. "Cleo! Figaro! Look who's here!" Geppetto was so pleased to see Pinocchio that he didn't notice his donkey ears and tail.

"I've come to save you," said Pinocchio, hugging his father tightly. "Let's get out of here!"

"I have made a raft, but it's hopeless," sighed Geppetto. "There's no way we can get out. Let's just make a fire and cook some fish."

"That's it!" cried Pinocchio. "A fire will make Monstro sneeze and blow us out! Hurry, Father! Bring more wood!"

The plan worked. As the smoke drifted towards Monstro's head, his giant body began to shake.

"Climb aboard, Father," cried Pinocchio, jumping onto the raft. They paddled towards the whale's mouth, but the way out was barred by its gigantic teeth.

Then suddenly Monstro gasped and let out an enormous sneeze. The raft was hurled into the ocean.

"We've made it!" shouted Pinocchio.

"Yes, but look – Monstro is angry!" cried Geppetto, pointing towards the whale as it came looming up behind them.

Monstro dived into the water, and his huge tail smashed onto the raft. Geppetto and Pinocchio were flung into the sea.

I spotted them in the distance and floated towards them.

"Save yourself, Pinocchio," gasped the old man, clinging to a plank of wood in the water.

But Pinocchio would not abandon his father. He swam up to him and pulled him towards the shore. Monstro plunged after us. Suddenly a huge wave surged onto the shore, sending Monstro crashing into the rocks.

When Geppetto opened his eyes he found himself on the seashore. Cleo, Figaro and I had miraculously survived, but Pinocchio was lying face down in the water.

"Oh, my brave little boy," sobbed Geppetto, lifting the lifeless body in his arms. He stumbled back to the village and put Pinocchio down on his bed.

Kneeling at the bedside, Geppetto buried his head in his arms, grief-stricken. He was too upset to notice a brilliant blue light filling the room. The Blue Fairy had come back.

Waving her magic wand over Pinocchio, she said, "Awake! You have proved yourself brave and unselfish. From this day, you will be a *real* boy!"

Pinocchio opened his eyes and sat up. "Father, what are you crying for?" he asked.

"Because you're dead!" sobbed Geppetto, not looking up.

"But Father, look! I'm alive – and I'm a real boy!" shouted Pinocchio, bouncing up and down.

Geppetto looked up and gasped with joy. Cleo and Figaro danced with excitement, and Geppetto, knowing that his dearest wish had been granted, felt he must be the happiest man alive.

Well, I could see that my job was done, and knew that it was time for me to leave. I packed my bag and went on my way.

So, that's the end of my story. And now you know why I believe that when you wish upon a star, your dreams come true!